The Robotx
Get Help from Simple Machines

Splitting Apart

The Wedge

Written by Gerry Bailey   Illustrated by Mike Spoor

The Robotx
Get Help from Simple Machines

Crabtree Publishing Company
www.crabtreebooks.com
1-800-387-7650

PMB 59051, 350 Fifth Ave.
59ᵗʰ Floor,
New York, NY 10118

616 Welland Ave.
St. Catharines, ON
L2M 5V6

Published by Crabtree Publishing in 2014

Author: Gerry Bailey
Illustrator: Mike Spoor
Editor: Kathy Middleton
Proofreader: Crystal Sikkens
End matter: Kylie Korneluk
**Production coordinator and
 Prepress technician:** Ken Wright
Print coordinator: Margaret Amy Salter

Copyright © 2013
BrambleKids Ltd.

Photographs:
All images are Shutterstock.com unless otherwise stated.
Pg 11 – tiorna
Pg 12 – Simon Krzic
Pg 13 – Ed Phillips
Pg 15 – bikeriderlondon
Pg 19 – apiguide
Pg 21 – (t) berna namoglu
Pg 21 (b) ason
Pg 23 – (l) enciktat (r) asife
Pg 25 – (t) KOO (b) Teri Virbickis
Pg 27 – ruigsantos

Printed in Canada/022014/MA20131220

Library and Archives Canada Cataloguing in Publication

Bailey, Gerry, author
        Splitting apart : the wedge / written by Gerry Bailey ; illustrated by Mike Spoor.

(The robotx get help from simple machines)
Includes index.
Issued in print and electronic formats.
ISBN 978-0-7787-0420-1 (bound).--ISBN 978-0-7787-0426-3 (pbk.).--ISBN 978-1-4271-7538-0 (pdf).--ISBN 978-1-4271-7532-8 (html)

        1. Wedges--Juvenile literature. I. Spoor, Mike, illustrator
II. Title.

TJ1201.W44B35 2014   j621.8   C2013-908717-6
                                                                      C2013-908718-4

Library of Congress Cataloging-in-Publication Data

Bailey, Gerry, author.
 Splitting apart : the wedge / written by Gerry Bailey ; illustrated by Mike Spoor.
      pages cm. -- (The Robotx get help from simple machines)
 Audience: Ages 5-8.
 Audience: K to grade 3.
 Includes index.
 ISBN 978-0-7787-0420-1 (reinforced library binding) -- ISBN 978-0-7787-0426-3 (pbk.) -- ISBN 978-1-4271-7538-0 (electronic pdf) -- ISBN 978-1-4271-7532-8 (electronic html)
1. Wedges--Juvenile literature. 2. Simple machines--Juvenile literature. I. Spoor, Mike, illustrator. II. Title. III. Title: Wedge.

TJ1201.W44B35 2014
621.8'11--dc23

                                                            2013050836

Contents

The Robotx

Meet   RobbO   and   RobbEE

The robots' workshop

It's snowing really hard outside. RobbO and RobbEE are watching from their workshop window.

The two robots find it hard to concentrate on making useful machines.

A machine is...

A machine is a tool used to make work easier. Work is the effort needed to create force. A force is a push or pull on an object. Machines allow us to push, pull, or lift a heavy weight much easier, or using less effort. All machines are made up of at least one **simple machine**.

There are six kinds of simple machines. Some have just one part that moves. Others are made up of two or more parts. The six simple machines are:

- **lever**
- **pulley**
- **inclined plane**
- **wheel and axle**
- **wedge**
- **screw**

In this book, the Robotx will help us learn all about the wedge.

Now the snow is really building up outside.

"I guess we'll be stuck here for a while," says RobbEE.

"The snow is too deep to walk in," agrees RobbO. "So, we'll just have to move it!"

"Move the snow!" says RobbEE. "But we can't..."

"Yes, we can!" says RobbO. "We just have to attach a wedge to the front of the tractor—two, in fact."

"Now we have—a snowplow.
Let's go and move some snow!"
cries RobbO.

RobbO and RobbEE jump on the tractor and drive out into the yard. The snowplow works perfectly, cutting into the snow and pushing it to either side of the tractor.

Soon the Robotx are on their way, cutting through the snow and leaving a clear path for pedestrians to walk along.

The wedge part of a snowplow is a kind of simple machine. It is actually two simple machines joined together. It's a double wedge.

The wedge

The wedge is made up of inclined planes. An inclined plane is a sloping surface, such as a ramp, that is used to a slide an object from a lower place to a higher place.

Moving an object using an inclined plane is easier than lifting an object to a higher place.

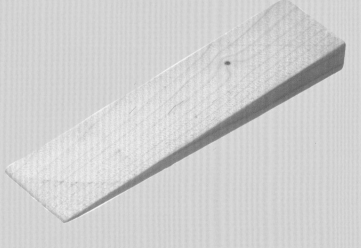

A wedge can be made up of one or two inclined planes. A single wedge is made up of one inclined plane. A doorstop is a single wedge that is used to hold a door still.

An inclined plane doesn't move, but a wedge can. When a wedge moves, it creates a sideways force that causes something to split or separate.

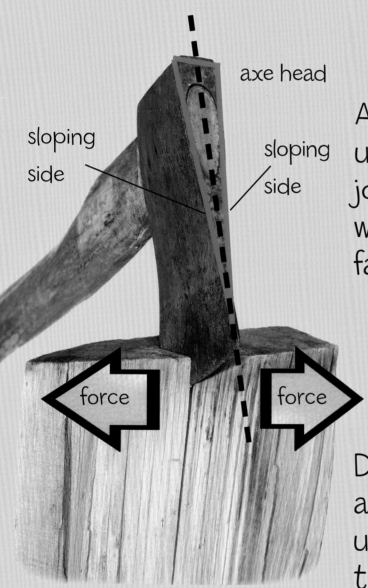

axe head

sloping side

sloping side

force

force

A double wedge is made up of two inclined planes joined together at a point with the sloping sides facing outward.

Double wedges, such as the axe head, are used to separate or split things. The axe head can be used to split wood.

Splitting wood

RobbEE and RobbO have cleared the snow away and they need to warm up. "Let's find some logs and light a fire," says RobbO.
He grabs a sharp axe.
As he swings the blade down, the force pushes the blade into the log, splitting it in two.
RobbEE helps with his axe.

The downward movement of the axe head is what produces the effort. It creates a splitting action that goes out sideways from the blade.

Monkey wedge

It's RobbEE's turn to tell a story as they sit around their fire.

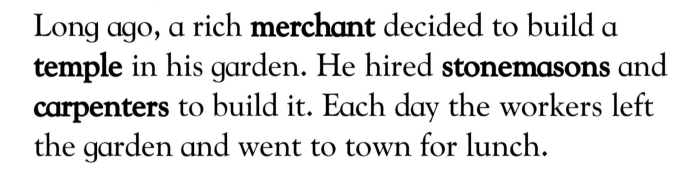

Long ago, a rich **merchant** decided to build a **temple** in his garden. He hired **stonemasons** and **carpenters** to build it. Each day the workers left the garden and went to town for lunch.

One day, when the workers were at lunch, a band of **mischievous** monkeys arrived in the garden. They began to play with whatever was lying around. One of the monkeys found a partly sawed log of wood. A wedge had been placed inside the cut to keep it from closing up.

The monkey became very curious. What exactly did the wedge do? Slowly at first, then much more quickly, he began to tug at the wedge. Finally, the wedge came loose. But as it did, the opening in the log slammed shut, trapping the monkey's nose.

The monkey yelled and yelled until finally a carpenter freed him.

The story has a **moral**.
"It's not wise," said the carpenter, "to poke your nose into other people's business."

Wedges at work

Knife

A knife is a kind of thin double wedge. The sharp side of the knife blade pushes into objects such as meat or bread and spreads them apart. This action is called cutting.

Chisel

A chisel is a tool with a long blade that ends in a very sharp wedge. It's used for carving or cutting wood or stone. Chisel blades are usually made of metal.

Zipper

A zipper is a device that uses wedges to open and close. Usually you find zippers on a pair of pants, a coat, or a bag. It is made up of two lower wedges that close and an upper wedge that opens.

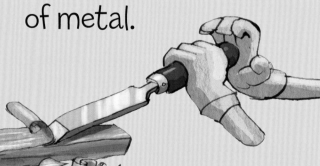

Saw

A saw has teeth and each tooth is a small wedge. Saw teeth actually tear things apart. The tearing action creates tiny bits of material called sawdust.

Scissors

Scissors have two simple machines that work together—a wedge and a lever.

The blades of the scissors are double wedges. Used together they slice objects apart.

Sheepshearing

Next, RobbO and RobbEE visit a sheep farm. The sheep are having their wool coats sheared, or cut off. First, they help **herd** the sheep into the shape of a wedge. That will help them fit more easily into their pen.

blade shears

Sheep are often raised for their wool. Once a year, usually in spring, their wool, or fleece, has to be removed. A special pair of scissors called blade shears are used. Unlike scissors, which are connected between the handle and the blades, blade shears are connected together at the top of the handle. Each blade is a sharp double wedge.

Rounded wedges

A double wedge doesn't have to have a flat blade. It can be rounded or come to a point.

Nail

A nail is a long, thin double wedge, ending in a point. When it is hit with a hammer into a piece of wood, the nail forces the wood apart, and the nail sinks into the wood.

Fork

A fork has a number of wedges at the end of a handle. These wedges dig into food and hold it.

Spoon

A spoon acts as a curved wedge to dig into soft food. The bowl of the spoon holds the food.

Your wedges

Did you know that you have some useful wedges on your body?

Your nails

Each of your nails is a kind of rounded wedge. Nails can be used to scrape or cut. Nails also protect the ends of your fingers.

Your teeth

Your two front teeth and the teeth on each side of them are shaped like flat wedges. They're called incisors and are used to cut or chop food. Beside the incisors are pointed teeth called canines. These wedges help tear food.

Birds that can cut

The Robotx are walking in the woods when they hear a tapping sound. A woodpecker is using its chisel-shaped beak to crack into the bark of a tree as it hunts for insects to eat.

The tapping is also a signal to other birds to stay away because this territory belongs to it.

Different birds have different-shaped beaks, but all beaks are wedges. They're used for different jobs, such as digging in the ground, tearing food apart, or for grooming.

Birds also have claws that are shaped like wedges. Birds, such as the eagle, that hunt small animals need sharp, curved claws to grab their food.

Two machines together

RobbO and RobbEE are digging into a pizza. RobbO divides it using a special pizza cutter.

"It's a super gadget," he says. "It's a double wedge, but it's also a wheel and axle. So it's two simple machines working together."

"Yummy..." says RobbEE, with his mouth full.

Flat iron

Flat irons were used long ago. These wedge-shaped appliances were filled with hot coals and used to iron clothing.

The Flatiron Building in New York City was given its name because of its   shape.

The wheel of a pizza cutter is attached to the handle by an axle. But the wheel is also a double wedge. It is wider at the center and gets narrower toward the edge until it becomes a thin cutting blade.

RobbO's science workshop

RobbO explains the wedge to his friends.

Although wedges are a kind of inclined plane, they are used for different work. Inclined planes are used to move objects from a lower place to a higher place. Wedges are used to hold things in place or separate things.

A wedge can be made up of one or two inclined planes. It's either a single wedge or a double wedge.

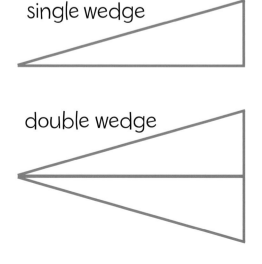

single wedge

double wedge

An axe is a double wedge. It has two inclined planes joined together. Their sloping surfaces come together to make a sharp blade that can separate things.

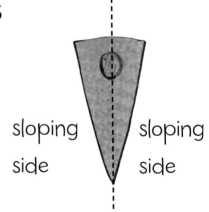

sloping side   sloping side

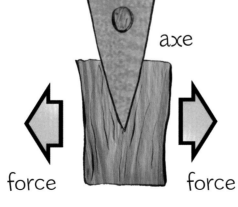

axe

force   force

An axe has a wedge that creates a sideways force that splits the wood apart.

Build a gnasher-masher

The Robotx think of another clever use for a wedge. This machine is a super-chopper that can crunch trash and other waste materials into small pieces. The wedges act like teeth, or gnashers as RobbEE calls them. Each wedge bites the waste into smaller and smaller pieces.

Learning more

Books

Get to Know: Wedges
By Jennifer Christiansen
(Crabtree Publishing, 2009)

Put Wedges to the Test
By Roseann Feldmann and Sally M. Walker
(Lerner Publishing, 2011)

How Toys Work: Ramps and Wedges
By Sian Smith
(Heinemann, 2012)

Websites

www.brainpop.com/technology/simplemachines
Activities based on the wedge and how it works.

www.mikids.com/Smachines.htm
Examples of what a wedge is and how it is used.

teacher.scholastic.com/dirtrep/Simple/wedge.htm
A short summary on what a wedge is and examples of how
it is used.

Glossary

carpenters People who build things using wood

herd A group of the same kind of animal

inclined plane A slanted surface connecting a lower point to a higher point

lever A bar that rests on a support called a fulcrum which lifts or moves loads

merchant A person who sells things

mischevious Being tricky or misbehaving

moral A lesson or meaning

pulley A simple machine that uses grooved wheels and a rope to raise, lower, or move a load

screw An inclined plane wrapped around a pole which holds things together or lifts materials

simple machine A machine that makes work easier by transferring force from one point to another

stonemasons People who build things using stones

temple A holy place; usually religious

wedge Two inclined planes joined together used to split things

wheel and axle A wheel with a rod, called an axle, through its center which lifts or moves loads

Index